Lola Fanola

Written by Penny Dolan
Illustrated by Bruno Robert

WAYLAND

Lola Fanola was the
star of Carlo's Circus.

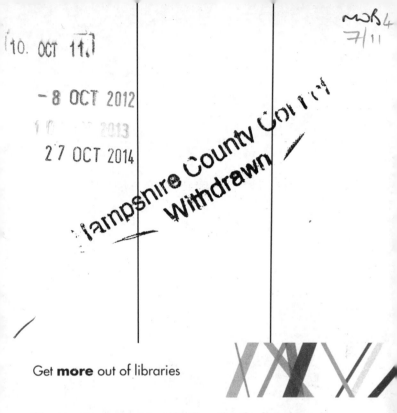

Get **more** out of libraries

Please return or renew this item by the last date shown.
You can renew online at www.hants.gov.uk/library
Or by phoning 0845 603 5631

Hampshire
County Council

Lola Fanola

First published in 2008
by Wayland

This paperback edition published in 2009
Reprinted in 2010

Text copyright © Penny Dolan 2008
Illustration copyright © Bruno Robert 2008

Wayland
338 Euston Road
London NW1 3BH

Wayland Australia
Level 17/207 Kent Street
Sydney, NSW 2000

The rights of Penny Dolan to be identified as the Author
and Bruno Robert to be identified as the Illustrator of this Work have
been asserted by them in accordance with the Copyright, Designs and
Patents Act, 1988.

Series Editor: Louise John
Editor: Katie Powell
Cover design: Paul Cherrill
Design: D.R.ink
Consultant: Shirley Bickler

A CIP catalogue record for this book is available from the British Library.

ISBN 9780750255363 (hbk)
ISBN 9780750255400 (pbk)

Printed in China

Wayland is a division of Hachette Children's Books,
an Hachette Livre UK Company

www.hachettelivre.co.uk

She swung on the
high trapeze.

5

But Lola made Jimmy swing
on the low trapeze.

She made him walk on the
long, low beam.

Lola walked along the high, high wire.

8

"Hooray for Lola Fanola!"
everyone cried.

9

"Let me swing on the high trapeze," said Jimmy. "Let me walk on the high wire. I can do it."

"No," said Lola. "I am the only star of the high trapeze!"

13

One day, just before their act,
Lola was hungry.

She ate a big, fat,
jammy doughnut!

As Lola danced and pranced on the high wire, a hungry wasp flew down.

It sat on the jam on Lola's nose.

"Help!" Lola cried.
She began to wobble.

Jimmy grabbed the
high trapeze.

"Hold on, Lola!" he cried. "I'm coming to get you!"

Jimmy swung out on the trapeze, and he grabbed Lola as she fell.

"Oooh!" went the crowd.

"You saved me, Jimmy," said Lola. "You are the star of the circus show today!"

23

START READING is a series of highly enjoyable books for beginner readers. **The books have been carefully graded to match the Book Bands widely used in schools.** This enables readers to be sure they choose books that match their own reading ability.

Look out for the Band colour on the book in our Start Reading logo.

The Bands are:

Pink Band 1

Red Band 2

Yellow Band 3

Blue Band 4

Green Band 5

Orange Band 6

Turquoise Band 7

Purple Band 8

Gold Band 9

START READING books can be read independently or shared with an adult. They promote the enjoyment of reading through satisfying stories supported by fun illustrations.

Penny Dolan had great fun writing about Carlo's Circus, because she could pretend she was an expert juggler, brave trapeze artist, cheeky clown and an amazing elephant rider – even though she's definitely not!

Bruno Robert lives and works in Normandy, France, where he was born. He always wanted to draw and play with colours. When he is illustrating a story like this one, he likes to think of a bright and colourful world that is full of humour.

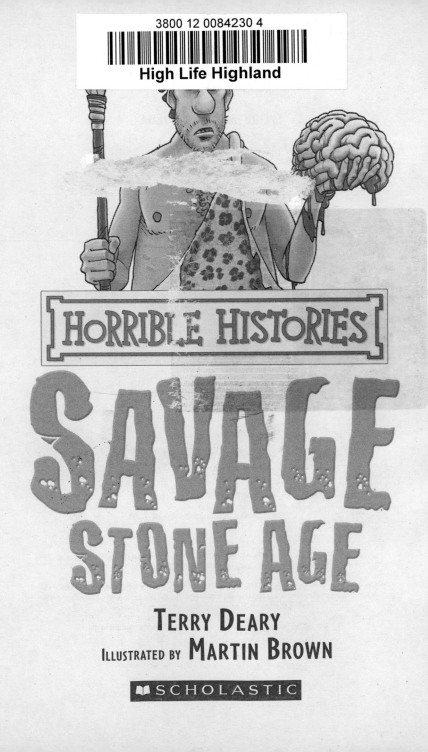

HORRIBLE HISTORIES

SAVAGE
STONE AGE

TERRY DEARY
ILLUSTRATED BY MARTIN BROWN

■SCHOLASTIC

To Erica Sheppard, with thanks

Scholastic Children's Books,
Euston House, 24 Eversholt Street,
London, NW1 1DB, UK

A division of Scholastic Ltd
London ~ New York ~ Toronto ~ Sydney ~ Auckland
Mexico City ~ New Delhi ~ Hong Kong

First published in the UK by Scholastic Ltd, 1999
This edition published 2008

Text copyright © Terry Deary, 1999
Illustrations © Martin Brown, 1999
All rights reserved

ISBN 978 1407 10428 7

Printed and bound by CPI Group (UK) Ltd, Croydon, CR0 4YY

19 20 18

The right of Terry Deary and Martin Brown to be identified as the author and illustrators of this work respectively has
been asserted by them in accordance with the Copyright, Designs and Patents Act, 1988.

Papers used by Scholastic Children's Books are made from wood grown in sustainable forests.

Contents